Learning to Read, Step by Step!

Ready to Read   Preschool–Kindergarten
• big type and easy words • rhyme and rhythm • picture clues
For children who know the alphabet and are eager to
begin reading.

Reading with Help   Preschool–Grade 1
• basic vocabulary • short sentences • simple stories
For children who recognize familiar words and sound out
new words with help.

Reading on Your Own   Grades 1–3
• engaging characters • easy-to-follow plots • popular topics
For children who are ready to read on their own.

Reading Paragraphs   Grades 2–3
• challenging vocabulary • short paragraphs • exciting stories
For newly independent readers who read simple sentences
with confidence.

Ready for Chapters   Grades 2–4
• chapters • longer paragraphs • full-color art
For children who want to take the plunge into chapter books
but still like colorful pictures.

STEP INTO READING® is designed to give every child a successful
reading experience. The grade levels are only guides; children will progress
through the steps at their own speed, developing confidence in their reading.

Remember, a lifetime love of reading starts with a single step!

Thomas the Tank Engine & Friends ™ CREATED BY BRITT ALLCROFT

Based on the Railway Series by the Reverend W Awdry.

© 2016, 2012 Gullane (Thomas) LLC.

Thomas the Tank Engine & Friends and Thomas & Friends are trademarks of Gullane (Thomas) Limited. Thomas the Tank Engine & Friends and Design Is Reg. U.S. Pat. & Tm. Off. © 2016 HIT Entertainment Limited. All rights reserved. Published in the United States by Random House Children's Books, a division of Penguin Random House LLC, 1745 Broadway, New York, NY 10019, and in Canada by Penguin Random House Canada Limited, Toronto. Originally published in different form in Great Britain by Egmont UK Ltd., as *The Tall Friend*, in 2012.

Step into Reading, Random House, and the Random House colophon are registered trademarks of Penguin Random House LLC.

Visit us on the Web!
StepIntoReading.com
randomhousekids.com
www.thomasandfriends.com

ISBN 978-1-101-94034-1 (trade) — ISBN 978-1-101-94035-8 (lib. bdg.) — ISBN 978-1-101-94036-5 (ebook)

Printed in the United States of America
10 9 8 7 6 5 4 3 2 1

Random House Children's Books supports the First Amendment and celebrates the right to read.

HIT entertainment

STEP INTO READING®

STEP 2

READING WITH HELP

THOMAS' TALL FRIEND

THOMAS & FRIENDS™

Based on the Railway Series
by the Reverend W Awdry

Random House 🏠 New York

Peep! Peep!

Edward carries apples.

Percy carries leaves.

The apples and leaves
are for the animal park.
Edward and Percy
head off!

Look!

An animal for the park.

It has a long neck.

It is a giraffe!

Thomas must take the giraffe to its new home.

Gordon tells
Thomas to wait
for the giraffe
keeper.
But Thomas
does not wait.
He puffs away!

Thomas tries to go under a bridge.

Oh, no!

The giraffe is too tall!

Thomas backs up.

Edward chuffs by.
Thomas wants
the giraffe to sit.

Thomas asks Edward for his apples.

The giraffe eats
the apples.

But the giraffe
does not sit!

Percy chuffs by.
Thomas asks Percy
for his leaves.

The giraffe
eats and eats.
It eats all
the leaves.

The giraffe is full.
It is sleepy. It sits!
Now the giraffe fits
under the bridge!

Thomas pulls up
to the animal park.
He has the giraffe
but no
giraffe food!
Sir Topham Hatt
is cross.

Thomas goes
to get more food.
He loads his cars
with apples and leaves.

Thomas puffs
all the way back
to the park.

The giraffe stretches
his long neck.

He gives his friend
Thomas a thank-you kiss!